The

HORNBILL KING

LEGACY OF THE CANOPY

By

Dinnis Thommachan

A Book By:

FOREVER SHININGS

Book Title: The Hornbill King: Legacy Of The Canopy

Book Author: Dinnis Thommachan

Published By: Forever Shinings

First Edition: 2026

ISBN: 978-93-7406-184-8

About the Book

THE HORNBILL KING: *The Legacy Of Canopy* is an epic fable of love, leadership, and resistance, told through the eyes of the forest itself. It is—a timeless story about finding strength in vulnerability, building power through community, and the courage to protect what you love, even when you are walled in darkness.

About the Author

This story was born not from ambition, but from stillness. It began on a path I had not planned—an unexpected creation, conceived in the quiet aftermath of a storm.

A recent battle with cancer and the transformative surgery that followed carved a permanent shift in my world. During this forced pause, in the liminal space between what was and what will be, this story emerged. These characters became my gentle companions in recovery, and I now offer them to you.

"For I know the plans I have for you," declares the LORD, "plans to prosper you and not to harm you, plans to give you hope

— Jeremiah 29:11

Thanks Note

This book was born in a season of stillness, a story that grew from the quiet soil of recovery. While my name is on the cover, it was nourished by the love and unwavering support of many.

My deepest gratitude goes to my siblings & my friends- You were my anchors, holding the pieces of my world together when I could not- My Eternal pillars .

To my extended family—relatives, aunts, uncles, and cousins—your collective embrace was a safety net. Every call, every message, every gesture of kindness was a thread of light in a challenging time.

To all my friends, who showed up with laughter, quiet understanding, and steadfast presence: you reminded me of the world beyond the storm. Thank you for walking this path beside me without flinching.

This story, and my journey through it, would not have been possible without you. Thank you for being my companions, not just in recovery, but in life.

With all my heart

Dedicated To

For every child who has ever looked up at a tree and wondered who lives there,

For every young heart that roots for the underbird,
And for every pair of eyes that still sees the wild not as a place to conquer, but as a story to join—

This tale of roots, wings, and the web that connects us all is for you.

May your adventures be wild, your friendships loyal, and your hearts forever tuned to the whisper of the leaves.

May you always find your flock, trust your own song, and protect the magic in your world.

With hope and wonder,

-Dinnis Thommachan.

-

Editorial Review

Hornbill King: Legacy of the Canopy is a standout achievement in animal fantasy. It transcends its premise to deliver a powerful, moving story about leadership, community, and the courage to build a different kind of kingdom. Dinnis Thommachan has crafted a world that is not only believable but aspirational, with a cast of characters whose struggles and triumphs resonate deeply.

Key Characters Of Hornbill King: Legacy Of The Canopy

THE HORNBILLS (HORNBILLIDAE)

The Royal Family

- **BAKUL (The Protagonist / King):**
    - **Trait:** Intelligent, earnest, and empathetic. Begins idealistic and untested, maturing into a wise, strategic leader who learns that true strength lies in connection.
    - **Symbol:** His casque is a vibrant sunset of orange and yellow. Represents his legacy of warmth and light.
    - **Arc:** From sheltered heir -> grieving, outcast king -> cunning "web-weaver" -> wise Guardian-King.
    - **Quote:** "The drongo cannot fight the eagle, but it can warn the forest."
- **BELA (The Queen / Strategist):**
    - **Trait:** Fiercely independent, pragmatic, observant, and deeply connected to the raw pulse of the forest. She is Bakul's equal and his moral compass.

  - **Symbol:** Her plumage is a deeper, luminous black; her casque is a smooth, elegant chestnut.
  - **Arc:** From solitary Guardian -> reluctant ally -> co-conspirator -> sealed Queen & mother -> co-ruler. Her time in the sealed nest is a crucible of faith.
  - **Quote:** "You don't fight a sword with a bigger sword. You fight it with a net."

- **PHALGUN (The Heir / Prince):**
  - **Trait:** Curious, brave, resilient. His growth from hatchling to fledgling mirrors the restoration of the kingdom. He is the hopeful future, raised in the new ways.
  - **Symbol:** His fledgling fluff, then his emerging casque. Named for the gentle spring wind.
  - **Arc:** From vulnerable chick in darkness -> witness to sacrifice and alliance -> eager student of the web -> potential future guardian.
  - **Quote:** "The weavers said the python is gone, father. Can I scout the ridge now?"

The Loyalists & Elders

- **GARUD (The Fallen King):**
  - **Trait:** Noble, wise, and burdened. A believer in the old unity, but perhaps too trusting of the stability he built.
  - **Symbol:** His majestic, powerful presence and his tragic, poisoned fall.
  - **Role:** Catalyst. His murder sets Bakul's journey in motion and leaves the cryptic clue of the "Heartwood Nest."
  - **Quote (Last Words):** "The… Heartwood… Nest… is not a… nest…"
- **KALA (The Usurper / Shadow):**
  - **Trait:** Powerful, brooding, cynical, and scarred by a worldview where only strength and survival matter. A tragic antagonist.
  - **Symbol:** His matte-black plumage, scarred casque, and dominion over the dark, misty Shadow Gorge.
  - **Arc:** From embittered exile -> challenger -> usurper of the north -> tyrannical ruler -> defeated rival -> redeemed Guardian of the Shadows.
  - **Quote:** "The fire culls the weak. The forest renews itself in ash. That is the true law."

- **VIHANGA (The Elder):**
    - **Trait:** Ancient, respected, and the living voice of tradition and law.
    - **Role:** The one who formally proclaims Bakul king after Garud's death. His sacrificial death defending Phalgun is a pivotal moment that hardens the flock's resolve.
    - **Quote:** "The lineage is clear. By sky and tree, by the old ways, Bakul, son of Garud, is king."

THE ALLIES (THE "WEB")

- **TAL (The Great Black Woodpecker):**
    - **Trait:** Gruff, taciturn, immensely knowledgeable. A historian of the forest's deep lore, valuing skill and efficiency.
    - **Symbol:** His chisel-like beak and jet-black, gem-like eyes.
    - **Role:** Bakul's reluctant mentor and chief cartographer. He deciphers the legend of the First Tree and provides crucial strategy.
    - **Quote:** "You swing like a blind monkey. The energy for ten figs, wasted on one."

- **THE DRONGO PAIR (Sentinels):**
    - **Trait:** Agile, fiercely territorial, brilliant mimics, and natural alarm systems.
    - **Symbol:** Their forked tails and daring, acrobatic dives.
    - **Role:** Become Bakul's early-warning network and communications hub. Their alliance is a practical trade: protection for intelligence.
    - **Quote:** (A complex, trilling call that means "Ridge guarded – falcons.")
- **MYNA (The Jungle Myna / Traitor):**
    - **Trait:** Sly, cunning, manipulative, and ambitious. A master of information and psychological warfare.
    - **Symbol:** His oily-smooth voice and constant, flitting movement.
    - **Role:** Garud's former advisor who orchestrates his murder and becomes Kala's vizier, only to ultimately betray him in a bid for his own power.
    - **Arc:** From whisperer -> king-maker -> betrayer -> exiled outcast.
    - **Quote:** "Perhaps the heir… could bridge this divide?" (Always posing as the helpful one.)

- **THE WEAVER BIRD COLONY:**
  - **Trait:** Communal, ingenious engineers, cheerful but vulnerable.
  - **Symbol:** Their intricate, hanging nests.
  - **Role:** Represent the small, productive citizens of the forest. Their protection from the kite is Bakul's first major act of practical kingship. They later provide logistics (carry-nets) and unconventional weaponry (sticky down).
  - **Quote (Chief Weaver):** "The kite may return. Our nests need stronger anchor lines."
- **THE LANGUR TROOP:**
  - **Trait:** Loud, communal, strong, and possessors of long memory and grudging respect for just rulers.
  - **Role:** Ground/Canopy allies who provide disruptive diversions, reconnaissance from the treetops, and sheer numbers.
  - **Symbol:** Their raucous alarm calls and ability to rain down debris.
- **THE ROCK PYTHON:**
  - **Trait:** Ancient, patient, and concerned solely with the balance of the ecosystem. An implacable, neutral force turned ally.

  - **Role:** A living barrier and symbol of primal, earthly power. His participation signifies that the conflict has disrupted the natural order itself.
  - **Quote (Hiss, translated):** "Chaos is bad for the hunt. Order serves all who wait."

THE ANTAGONISTS' FORCES

- **KALA'S FACTION:** Carrion Crows (bullies, mockers), Shrikes ("butcher birds," enforcers), Brown Fish Owls (silent assassins), Shikras & Falcons (aerial shock troops), Wild Dogs/Jackals (ground muscle).
- **THE SKIN-TAKERS (Humans / Poachers):** The existential external threat. They represent chaos, greed, and the "thunder-stick" – a force against which traditional animal conflict is meaningless, requiring ultimate unity to outsmart.

THE SETTING AS CHARACTER

- **THE SUNDARBAN (The Beautiful Forest):** The lush, biodiverse Western Ghats. It is the kingdom, the prize, and the entity that must be healed.
- **THE FIRST TREE (The Heartwood Nest):** The ancient, cathedral-like Banyan. It is the moral and spiritual heart of the forest, the source of legitimacy and the symbol of interconnected life.

- **THE SHADOW GORGE:** Kala's domain. A place of mist, deep shadows, carrion, and forgotten secrets. Represents the repressed, harsh aspects of the wild that must be integrated, not conquered.
- **THE VALLEY OF ECHOES:** Bela's home. A place of mystery, refuge, and strange acoustics. Represents the hidden wisdom and alternative perspectives that Bakul must embrace to become a true king.

Prologue: The Seal

The mud was the color of dried blood, and it held the future.

Bela pressed the last beakful into the narrow slit of the world, her movements precise, ritualistic. From the outside, the great *sal* tree was just another giant in a forest of giants. But inside its heart, a miracle was incubating. As the opening narrowed to a finger-width, the cacophony of the Western Ghats—the shriek of langurs, the whisper of a million leaves, the distant thunder of the monsoon gathering its breath—faded to a muffled symphony. Soon, there would be only darkness, the rustle of her own feathers, and the faint, precious tapping from within the single, large egg nestled against her breast.

Her final act before the seal closed completely was to look out. Through the vertical slit, she saw a fragment of her world: a tapestry of emerald canopy, a slash of monsoon-grey sky, and *him*.

Bakul stood sentinel on a nearby branch, his silhouette a monument of black and gold against the brewing storm. His great casque, a curved sword of keratin, gleamed even in the diffuse light. His eyes, bright as river-polished amber, were fixed on her. In them, she saw not just the duty of a mate, but the weight of a king. A king whose throne was trembling.

She uttered a soft, guttural *gok*—a sound that meant *I trust you. I am here. We are.*

He dipped his magnificent beak in acknowledgment, a regal nod. Then, with a powerful downstroke that scattered leaves, he was gone, a black-and-white comet shooting into the gloom. His mission: to feed a kingdom and a family, alone, for the moons it would take their chick to grow.

The mud dried. The slit became a line, then a scar. Darkness, warm and complete, embraced her.

In the silence, Bela felt the immensity of it. She was queen of the Sundarban, the Beautiful Forest, and she was sealed in a tomb of wood. Her life, and the life of the heir she carried, depended entirely on the strength of the wings she could no longer use, on the loyalty of a parliament of birds fracturing into discord, and on the love of a king whose crown was being pulled from his head by shadows.

The egg pulsed with warmth against her skin.

Somewhere far away, thunder growled. Not the thunder of rain, but the thunder of coming war.

Index

Part 3:
The Heartwood Ascendant

Part 1:

The Heir And The Hollow

Chapter 1: The Parliament of Wings

The Grand Fig was in riotous fruit, a crimson beacon in the sea of green. It should have been a time of plenty, of celebration. Instead, the air crackled with tension.

Bakul perched beside his father, King Garud, on the highest branch of the Council Fig, the ancient tree that had borne witness to a hundred generations of hornbill kings. Below them, on a carefully arranged architecture of branches, sat the Parliament of the Sundarban.

It was a breathtaking, dizzying spectacle. Closest to the throne were the **High Perch**: the other hornbills—the smaller Malabar greys, the elegant Malabar pieds—their casques glowing in the dappled light. Next, the **Eyes of the Sky**: the hawk-eagles and serpent eagles, regal and fierce, their gazes missing nothing. The **Wardens of the Bark**: a line of great black woodpeckers, like living obsidian. The **Living Jewels**: shimmering flocks of sunbirds and fairy-bluebirds. The **Cynics**: a murmuration of jungle mynas, led by the sharp-beaked Myna, who seemed to be everywhere at once, whispering. Farther out were the **Ground-Walkers**: the painted storks on long, stilt-like legs, the pragmatic junglefowl. And at the very edges, perched in the shadows of thick foliage, were the **Watchers from the Dark**: a contingent of silent, broad-faced brown wood owls, and a single, immense shape that made the air grow cold—Kala.

Bakul's uncle. Garud's estranged brother. Lord of the Shadow Gorge.

"The northern marshes burn!" The cry came from a painted stork, his usually pristine feathers smudged with soot. "The Smoke-Stones of the Skin-Takers have turned our nesting grounds to ash! Our eggs are cooked in the shells!"

A ripple of horror went through the Parliament. The storks were not warriors, but they were elders, symbols of grace.

Garud raised a wing, and the forest fell silent but for the wind. His voice was a deep, resonant *gronk* that carried to the furthest watcher. "The Sundarban does not abandon its own. The fire is a wound on the body of us all. We will aid our brothers. We will share our groves for nesting. We will—"

"We will weaken ourselves for sentiment." The voice was like stone grinding on stone. Kala shifted in the shadows. He was larger than Garud, his plumage a deeper, more matte black, his casque scarred and notched from forgotten battles. His eyes held no amber warmth, only a flat, calculating darkness. "The fire culls the weak. The forest renews itself in ash. Let the storks adapt or perish. That is the true law. Not this… *Accord*." He spat the last word.

Bakul felt a hot flash of anger. "The Accord is what keeps the leopards from picking us off one by one! It is what warns the woodpeckers of the slithering ones! It is our strength!"

Kala's gaze slid to Bakul, dismissive. "The pup barks the father's words. Have you ever seen fire, little prince? Have you ever hunted in the Scarred Hills, where the wind screams? Have you ever sealed a mate in a tree, knowing a python waits in the roots?" He leaned forward. "You learn the forest from a throne, not from the talons."

The insult was direct, a challenge to Bakul's worthiness. Before Bakul could retort, Myna fluttered to a central branch, his voice oily-smooth. "Great Kala speaks of harsh truths, but King Garud speaks of great compassion. Perhaps the heir… could bridge this divide? Let Prince Bakul lead a scouting flight to the northern marshes. Let him see the nature of this threat. A king should know his entire kingdom, not just its heart."

It sounded reasonable. Noble, even. But Bakul saw the glint in Myna's eyes. It was a trap. He was untested. If he failed, his credibility would shatter.

Garud looked at his son, his old eyes filled with a complex mixture of pride and fear. He knew the trap as well. But to refuse would be a greater weakness. "The suggestion has merit," Garud said slowly. "Bakul will go. He will see, and he will report. The Parliament will reconvene at the next full moon."

As the assembly broke into a cacophony of chatter, Kala locked eyes with Bakul one last time. "Try not to get lost, nephew," he rumbled, before melting back into the forest shadows.

Chapter 2: The Storm and the Stranger

Bakul's scouting party was small: two loyal Malabar grey hornbills as his wing-guards, and a pair of sharp-eyed drongos as scouts. They flew north for a day, the lush green of the central Sundarban giving way to drier, rockier slopes. The air grew acrid.

The sight of the marshlands struck Bakul mute. It was a charred nightmare. Ancient, moss-hung trees stood as blackened skeletons against a grim sky. The air tasted of ash. The comforting chorus of insects and frogs was replaced by an eerie silence, broken only by the desperate cries of a few surviving storks picking through the ruins.

"It… it is all gone," one of the grey hornbills whispered, aghast.

The drongos, flitting over the scorched earth, returned with grim news. "The fire did not walk like a natural fire," one reported. "It started in many places at once. And see here…" It pointed its beak at the ground. Pressed into the soft mud at the edge of the blackness was a print Bakul had only heard of in warnings: a five-toed, heeled print. **Skin-Taker.**

A cold dread, deeper than any fear of Kala, settled in Bakul's gizzard. This was no accident. It was an attack.

On the flight back, the monsoon, which had been threatening for days, finally broke. It wasn't gentle rain; it was a furious, grey wall of water. The wind tore at his wings, turning the world into a disorienting whirl of water and shaking leaves. His guards were blown off course. The drongos vanished into the gloom.

Alone, battered, Bakul fought the storm. He was a powerful flier, but this was the fury of the Ghats unleashed. A vicious gust slammed him into the canopy. Branches, like skeletal hands, scraped his wings. He tumbled, a cascade of black, white, and gold, through a curtain of vines and into a place the maps in his mind did not know.

He crash-landed in a soft bed of moss and rotting leaves, the wind knocked from him. Pain flared in his right wing. He was in a deep, narrow valley, so thick with mist and towering, strange trees that the storm above was just a distant roar. The air was cool, heavy with the scent of damp earth and unknown flowers. This was the **Valley of Echoes**. The forbidden place. His father's stern warning echoed in his mind: *"No hornbill flies there. It is a place of old magic and older sorrows."*

As he struggled to rise, a shadow detached itself from a nearby *palaquium* tree. It was a hornbill. A female. But unlike any he had seen. She was slightly smaller, her plumage a richer, deeper jet, and her casque was a smooth, elegant helm of burnt umber, unadorned by the carvings of battle. She looked at him not with fear or deference, but with keen, analytical curiosity.

“You fly like a rock with feathers,” she said, her voice a clear, crisp *kok*. “And you’re in my tracking path.”

Bakul, heir to the Sundarban, could only stare, water dripping from his casque. “I am Bakul. Son of Garud.”

The female cocked her head. “I am Bela. Daughter of the Valley. And your title means nothing to the mud on your back. Can you stand, Son of Garud, or will you be a feast for the beetles?”

Chapter 3: Lessons in the Green Dark

Bela was a creature of silent footfalls and supreme competence. She showed him how to chew a particular fern to make a poultice for his bruised wing. She found him grubs fat as his talon in places he would have overlooked. She moved through the Valley of Echoes not as a visitor, but as a part of its very breath.

He learned why it was forbidden. The valley was a labyrinth of sheer cliffs and deep gorges, where sound behaved strangely. A call from here would echo from there, disorienting predators and travelers alike. It was also the last refuge of creatures rarely seen: the shy, nocturnal slender loris, the brilliant but reclusive Malabar trogon.

"My father was Guardian here," Bela said one evening as they shared a fig. "Alone. He believed the old stories—that this valley holds the First Sapling from which all Sundarban grew. He died keeping a leopard pair from denning here." There was no self-pity in her voice, only fierce pride. "Now I am the Guardian."

Bakul, accustomed to the politics of the Parliament, was fascinated by her solitary, direct world. He told her of the burning marshes, of Kala's challenge, of the Skin-Taker print.

Bela's eyes grew hard. "The Skin-Takers have been here too. They come for the trogon feathers, for the loris. They set snares of invisible vine that bite." She led him to a clearing where a young sambar deer lay dead, its leg hideously swollen. "They poison the water holes sometimes. Their fire is just another weapon."

For the first time, Bakul saw the threat not as a political problem for his father, but as a visceral, existential war. "We must fight them," he said, the heat of kingship returning to his voice.

Bela gave him a look that was almost pitying. "Fight? With your beaks against their thunder-sticks? You cannot fight a flood, Bakul. You must learn to channel it. Or outsmart it."

She decided to show him. Using her knowledge of the echoes, she led him on a stalk. They found two Skin-Takers, moving through the undergrowth with clumsy noise. Bela didn't attack. She flew to a high cliff above them and gave a perfect mimic of a leopard's cough, throwing her voice using the echo walls. The men froze, panic on their faces. She then flew to the other side and mimicked the warning bark of a alarmed deer. The men, believing they were surrounded, turned and fled, dropping one of their strange, shiny snares.

Bakul watched, awestruck. This was a different kind of power. Not the power of the throne, but the power of the forest itself. In that moment, something shifted in him.

His admiration for Bela kindled into something warmer, brighter. He saw not just a competent guardian, but a spirit as wild and essential as the valley she protected.

And Bela, who had known only duty and solitude, looked at the bedraggled, earnest prince and saw not just a title, but a heart that could learn. A heart that could, perhaps, be trusted.

Chapter 4:
The Poisoned Branch

When Bakul finally returned to the Council Fig, guided by Bela who insisted on seeing him to the valley's edge, he was a changed bird. He carried not just the news of the deliberate fire, but a new quiet certainty. Bela stayed hidden in the canopy, watching.

The Parliament was reconvened. Garud listened gravely as Bakul delivered his report, his voice firm. "The fire was set. By Skin-Takers. It is a declaration of war not just on the storks, but on the Accord itself. They seek to break us by picking us apart."

Kala was there, a storm cloud on his perch. "So," he boomed, "the prince returns from his adventure with a tale of monsters. And his solution? More speeches? More sharing of nests? The Skin-Takers have thunder that kills from afar. What is talk against that?"

"Unity is our thunder," Bakul shot back, echoing Bela's lesson without naming her. "The drongo cannot fight the eagle, but it can warn the forest. The woodpecker cannot fight the python, but it can riddle its home with holes. Alone, we are prey. Together, we are the Sundarban."

His words, forged in the Valley of Echoes, rang with a conviction that silenced the murmuring mynas. Even some of the watchers from the dark seemed to lean forward.

Garud's eyes shone with pride. "The heir has seen, and he has learned. The Accord stands. We will—"

It was then that Myna made his move. He had been quietly observing, calculating. Bakul's successful return and newfound authority threatened his careful plans to erode the hornbill rule. He had already pledged his network of spies to Kala, promising him the throne in exchange for power in the new order.

As Garud spoke, Myna gave a subtle, pre-arranged signal to a gang of common mynas hidden in the foliage directly above the king's perch. They had spent days weakening a heavy, dead branch with their sharp beaks, daubing its splintered end with the toxic sap of the *nux vomica* tree.

Just as Garud raised his wing for emphasis, the mynas gave one final, coordinated push.

"—protect our own!" Garud finished.

The branch, thick as a python, cracked and fell.

It happened with nightmarish slowness. Bakul saw it. He screamed a warning. But Garud, old and focused on his speech, was too slow. The branch struck his left wing and shoulder with a sickening thud, the poisoned splinters digging deep before it clattered to the forest floor.

A collective gasp, a shriek of ten thousand birds, tore through the Fig.

Garud staggered, his majestic wing hanging at a wrong angle. His eyes met Bakul's, filled not with pain, but with a terrible urgency. He tried to speak, but a toxin-induced paralysis was already seizing his muscles. He managed one choked, guttural sound as Bakul rushed to his side.

"The… Heartwood… Nest… is not a… nest…"

Then his eyes, the amber lights that had guided the Sundarban for a generation, dimmed. His great body went limp.

Silence, absolute and deafening, swallowed the forest.

Kala's voice cut through it, cold and triumphant. "The old king is dead. Felled by a rotten branch. A sign. His time is over." He spread his vast wings, casting a pall over the assembly. "The strong must lead. I claim the throne by right of blood and strength. Who challenges?"

Bakul, cradling his father's head, looked up. Grief, white-hot and blinding, warred with a fury he had never known. He saw Myna, trying to look somber, but unable to hide the glint of satisfaction. He saw the fear in the eyes of the small birds. He saw the predatory interest in the eyes of Kala's allies.

He was no longer just the heir. He was the king. And his first act as king was to look at his murderous uncle and utter a single, resonant word that carried across the frozen Parliament.

"I do."

Part 2:

The Sealed Throne & The Small Allies

Chapter 5:
The Hollow Crown

The rain fell like tears on the Council Fig. It washed the pollen from the leaves, diluted the sap weeping from wounded bark, but could not cleanse the air of betrayal.

Bakul stood where his father had fallen. The body of King Garud had been borne away by the elder hornbills to the Crest of Passing, where the winds would carry his feathers to the four directions. But the ghost of the branch remained—a pale, jagged scar on the branch below the throne-perch.

Myna's voice, slick as oil on water, cut through the murmur of the stunned Parliament. "A tragic accident! The storms have weakened our oldest trees. Even the mighty can fall to time." His beady eyes swept the assembly, gauging, manipulating. "But the forest cannot mourn forever. The Sundarban needs a strong wing to lead it. Prince Kala stands ready."

Kala emerged from the shadows, not with a rush, but with a slow, inevitable unfolding of wings that seemed to drink the light. He did not look at Bakul, kneeling by the scarred wood. He addressed the birds, his voice the grating of tectonic plates.

"My brother spoke of Accords. Of unity. Look where it led him. To a fall. The Skin-Takers grow bold.

The weak," his gaze flicked to the painted storks, huddled and soot-stained, "expect the strong to bleed for them. No more. I offer not talk, but protection. I offer not sharing, but strength. Those who are strong will have a place beside me. The rest… will learn their place."

A chill settled over the Fig. The eagle clans shifted, their talons flexing in consideration. The myna flock chattered excitedly. The small birds—the sunbirds, the flowerpeckers—shrank into themselves, their vibrant colors seeming to dim.

Bakul rose. His legs felt like sapling wood, but he forced them straight. The grief was a physical weight in his crop, but beneath it, cooling and hardening like volcanic glass, was fury. He locked eyes with Myna, and for a fleeting second, the advisor flinched, seeing not a grieving son, but a king awakening.

"My father was not felled by time," Bakul said, his voice quieter than Kala's, but cutting through the drizzle with shocking clarity. "He was felled by treachery. And a kingdom built on treachery is a nest built on a serpent's back."

Kala finally looked at him, a dismissive smirk on his powerful beak. "Pretty words, pup. Can words stop a leopard? Can speeches seal a nest? You are a child playing with a crown of twigs."

The ancient hornbill elder, **Vihanga**, whose casque was pale with age, fluttered forward. His voice was thin but revered. “The lineage is clear. By sky and tree, by the old ways, Bakul, son of Garud, is king.”

A tense silence followed. It was a statement of law, not of power.

Kala’s eyes narrowed. He had expected a challenge he could crush in open combat, not this brittle formality. “The old ways,” he rumbled. “Let them be. Rule your heartwood, *nephew*. See how far your lineage carries you when the rains stop and the fruit is scarce. I will rule the north, the east, the Shadow Gorge. We will see which forest the birds choose when winter comes.”

It was not a concession. It was a partition. A declaration of civil war.

Without another word, Kala launched himself from the branch, a dark comet heading north. His followers—the shrikes, the carrion crows, the larger falcons, and a troubling number of common hornbills swayed by his rhetoric of power—flowed after him in a ragged, noisy stream.

The Parliament shattered, not with a bang, but with the rustle of a thousand wings taking flight in different directions.

Bakul was left standing on the Council Fig with the loyalists: the grieving storks, the nervous pigeons, a handful of old-guard hornbills, and the vast, silent majority of small birds who watched him with anxious, unblinking eyes.

He was king. And his kingdom had just been halved.

Chapter 6: The Guardian's Choice

He found her where he knew he would—at the border of the Valley of Echoes, perched on the lightning-struck *palaquium* where they had first truly spoken. Bela was preening, a picture of focused calm, but he saw the tension in the set of her wings.

She didn't look at him as he landed heavily beside her. "So. The King of Half a Forest."

The title, coming from her, didn't sting. It was just a fact. "The king of a forest with a knife at its throat," he replied, exhaustion seeping into his bones.

Now she looked at him. She took in the dried mud on his plumage from kneeling, the new, grim set of his jaw, the hollows grief had carved near his eyes. The sharp mockery in her own gaze softened, replaced by that analytical assessment. "What will you do?"

"What my father would have done," he said, but the words felt hollow. Garud's ways had led to a poisoned branch. He shook his great head, casque scraping bark. "I don't know, Bela. Kala offers simplicity. Strength. It is a lie, but it is an easy one to swallow."

"Easy for the strong to swallow," Bela corrected, turning to look out over her mist-shrouded valley. "For the drongo, the sunbird, the warbler… it is a death sentence.

Kala's world has no room for those who cannot fight for perches." She was silent for a long moment, listening to the echo of a distant waterfall. "My father believed a guardian's duty was to the land itself. To the balance. Not to a single flock or species." She turned her bright eyes back to him. "Your Accord… it is an attempt to be guardian of a balance, not just a king of hornbills. Isn't it?"

Her words named the elusive truth he'd been grappling with. "Yes," he said, the conviction solidifying. "But how do I protect a balance when the other side has all the swords?"

A ghost of her old smirk returned. "You don't fight a sword with a bigger sword. You fight it with a net. Or a mirror. Or by removing the ground from under its feet." She hopped closer, her voice dropping. "Kala sees the forest as a hierarchy. A pyramid with him at the top. You must see it as my valley sees it. A web. And in a web," she tapped his chest lightly with her beak, "every connection matters. Even the smallest strand can feel the tremors of the farthest fly."

The idea was a spark in the gloom. He had been thinking like a hornbill king. He needed to think like the Sundarban itself.

"Will you help me?" The question left him before he could weigh it. It was not a king's command. It was a plea.

Bela studied him again, longer this time. She looked past the crown he didn't yet wear, to the bird who had listened in her valley, who had been humbled by mud and saved by her wit. She saw the potential for a guardian-king.

"My valley is part of your Sundarban," she said finally, her tone decisive. "And the Skin-Takers who burn marshes will not stop at its borders. My fight is your fight." She paused, and a new, profound seriousness entered her gaze. "And a king needs a queen. Not for ceremony. For a seal."

He understood. The most powerful symbol a hornbill king could offer in a time of chaos was not a show of force, but a show of ultimate commitment, of future hope. The nesting ritual.

"It will make you a target," he said, his heart swelling with a mixture of love and dread. "Sealed and vulnerable."

"It will make *us* a fortress," she corrected. "A promise of tomorrow that Kala cannot offer. He rules by fear of loss. We will rule by promise of life. But," she added, her practical nature reasserting itself, "you must choose the tree wisely. And you must learn to rule while I am within it. You must learn to listen to the web."

Chapter 7: The Fortress Tree

They chose the **King's Sal**, a monarch of a tree that stood in a small, defensible clearing near a constant stream. It was old, its wood hard as iron, its trunk thick enough to deter any python. The entrance hole was high, facing east to catch the morning sun, and had a clear line of sight from several tall sentinel trees.

The work of preparing the nest was their last shared act before the long separation. They scraped and cleaned the deep chamber together, their beaks moving in synchronized rhythm. Bela lined the floor with the softest moss and dry, aromatic leaves Bakul brought—*jamun* leaves for their sweetness, *neem* for keeping pests away. There was a sacred intimacy to the labor, a silent conversation of touches and shared glances that wove their bond tighter than any vine.

Word spread through the loyalist lands. *The king is taking a queen. The line will continue.* It was a subtle, powerful counter to Kala's narrative of decay. Birds came to watch from a respectful distance—not just hornbills, but curious bulbuls, nervous squirrel families, a silent pair of mongooses from the undergrowth.

On the morning of the sealing, Bela stood at the entrance.

The Parliament of the loyal was gathered in the surrounding trees, a quieter, more somber assembly than the grand Fig. Bakul faced her, the forest holding its breath.

"I will keep the web," he promised, his forehead touching hers.

"And I will keep the heart," she replied, her voice steady.

Then she turned and entered the darkness. The last thing the outside world saw was the flash of her intelligent eye through the slit. Then began the rhythmic, wet sounds of sealing. Mud, dung, pulp. A prison. A womb. A fortress.

When it was done, and only a narrow vertical slit remained, Bakul felt a severing so profound it was physical. His other half, his strategist, his heart, was gone, walled away by her own will. The weight of his solitude crashed upon him.

It was then that the first taunt came. A harsh, laughing caw from the edge of the clearing.

A large carrion crow, one of Kala's, perched on a dead branch. "Look! The mighty king! Already he fails his first duty! How will he feed his mate, little prince? Will you beg berries from the babblers?"

Laughter echoed from other crows hidden in the foliage.

Bakul's instinct was a red-hot surge to attack, to drive them off with beak and fury. But he remembered Bela's words. *See the web.* He saw the crow.

But he also saw, in his periphery, a family of striped squirrels frozen on their trunk, watching. He saw a pair of red-whiskered bulbuls fall silent in a bush. They were waiting to see what kind of king he would be.

He did not charge the crow. Instead, he turned his back to it, a gesture of utter contempt, and addressed the squirrel family, his voice calm and clear. "The clearing is under the protection of the Crown. All who live here in peace share in its bounty. The *ficus* by the stream is heavy with fruit. It is for all."

Then, without another glance at the sputtering crow, he took off on his first foraging run as a working king. The message was delivered: he would not be drawn into Kala's petty games. He had work to do.

But as he flew, the loneliness was a vast, empty sky around him.

Chapter 8: The Take-Away King

The next moon was the hardest of Bakul's life. His days became a relentless, exhausting circuit. Dawn: deliver food to the slit (Bela's beak appearing, the brief, tender touch, her whispered reports of the chick's growth—a single, precious egg laid and now warming). Morning: forage for the next delivery, his throat pouch stretched and aching. Afternoon: attempt to "rule"—to show himself in the loyal groves, to listen to disputes between parakeet clans over a nesting palm, to reassure the ground-dwellers. Evening: more foraging, a final delivery to Bela, then a fitful sleep on a branch near the *sal* tree, one eye open.

Kala's mockery was constant. His crows and shrikes coined the name that spread like a fungus: **"The Take-Away King."** They would shadow Bakul on his foraging flights, cawing. "Making a delivery? Don't forget the grubs for the queen! Does she want a side of berries?" They stole fruit from under his beak, harassed the smaller birds who tried to help him.

Bakul's old-guard hornbill advisors urged retaliation. "Raise a flock! Drive them from the skies!" But Bakul had no flock to raise, and open war was what Kala wanted. It would be a slaughter.

He was failing. He knew it. He was thin, his plumage growing dull. Bela, from her slit, could sense his despair. Her calls grew more insistent, not for food, but for news. "Tell me of the forest, Bakul. Not the battles. The life."

One desperate afternoon, chasing a fat grub in a rotting log, he disturbed a nest of furious hornets. They swarmed him, a stinging, burning cloud. He fled, crashing through branches, finally plunging into a muddy forest pool to escape. He emerged, bedraggled, stung, the grub lost. Perching on a stone, humiliation washed over him. The Take-Away King, bested by insects.

A small, chittering sound made him look up. A **jungle striped squirrel** sat on a root, its tail twitching. It was the same one from the clearing.

"Stings need mud," it squeaked, then gestured with its nose to a particular blue-tinged clay at the pool's edge. "That kind. Not the brown."

Bakul, too weary for pride, hobbled over and applied the cool clay to his welts. The relief was immediate.

"Why help me?" he asked the squirrel.

The squirrel cocked its head. "You said the *ficus* was for all. The crows would have taken it all. You kept your word." It scampered away, but the act, small and unexpected, was a lifeline.

The next day, foraging for figs, he was struggling to break into a particularly tough-skinned cluster. A tap-tap-tap made him turn.

A **great black woodpecker**, a formidable bird with a beak like a chisel and eyes like black gems, watched him from a nearby trunk. This was **Tal**.

"You swing like a blind monkey," Tal stated, his voice a dry rattle. "The energy for ten figs, wasted on one." With two precise, powerful strikes, Tal split the fig cluster open, revealing the sweet red flesh inside. He took one seed for himself and flew off without another word.

Bakul stared at the opened fruit, then at the retreating woodpecker. It wasn't an act of loyalty. It was an act of professional disdain. But it was also… help.

That evening, at the slit, he told Bela not just of his failure with the hornets, but of the squirrel's clay and the woodpecker's efficiency. He expected pity.

Instead, he heard a soft, warm chuckle from the dark. "The web," Bela whispered, her voice full of hope. "You felt it. The smallest strand. Now *follow* it."

Chapter 9: The Council of Beaks

Following the strand led Bakul to the **Weaver Colony**—a hundred intricate, pendulous nests hanging like strange fruit over a quiet oxbow lake. The air was filled with the cheerful chatter of **baya weavers**. But today, the chatter was shrill with panic.

A **black kite**, a sleek, opportunistic hunter, was making lazy circles above the colony. Every so often, it would dive, not to catch a weaver, but to snatch mouthfuls of the precious long grasses from their half-built nests, scattering the builders. The weavers were too small to fight it, and rebuilding was draining them before the nesting season.

Bakul landed on a tall papyrus stalk. The kite saw him immediately and swooped closer, its eyes challenging. "Away, Take-Away King. This is my hunting sky."

The old Bakul might have risen to the challenge. The new Bakul, remembering the squirrel and the woodpecker, thought of the web. He thought of Bela in her dark chamber, trusting him to be clever.

He did not confront the kite. Instead, he flew, not at the kite, but north, toward the marshy edges where the fire had been. He returned minutes later, not with aggression, but with information.

He perched between the kite and the weaver colony. “Your hunting sky is poor,” Bakul called to the kite, his voice calm. “The fire stirred the rodents from the blackened earth. The hunting at the marsh edge is easy. Fat, slow mice, blinded by smoke. Why waste energy terrorizing weavers for grass, when a feast waits where you are not expected?”

The kite halted in mid-air, suspicion warring with hunger. It knew the marshes were contested, near Kala’s territory. “A trick to draw me away.”

Bakul shrugged a wing. “Stay. Pluck grass. I will go and tell the marsh hawks that the pickings are easy. They are always hungry.” He made as if to fly north again.

The kite hesitated, then with a disdainful shriek, it wheeled away from the weavers and shot toward the marshes. The weavers erupted in a chorus of grateful chirps.

Bakul didn’t stop. He flew to the weaver’s chief, a grizzled old male with a particularly ornate nest. “The kite may return. Your nests need stronger anchor lines. The vines by the western cliff are tough as sinew. But the cliff is watched by a pair of **drongos** who chase all comers.”

The weaver chief nodded eagerly. “We know the vines! But the drongos…”

“I will speak to the drongos,” Bakul said. An idea, fragile and new, was forming. “Tell your colony: the King’s protection is not a hornbill’s shadow over you.

It is a promise that your needs will be heard, and your enemies will become my concern."

It was a different kind of rulership. Transactional, perhaps. But it was real.

He found the drongo pair—agile, fiercely territorial birds with forked tails. They were notorious for mobbing any intruder, including eagles. They watched him land with hostile, gleaming eyes.

"The weavers need the cliff vines," Bakul said, dispensing with ceremony. "In return, they will leave the best of the insect swarms over the lake for you to hunt. They will also," he added, the idea crystallizing, "be your eyes. A hundred eyes, scattered through the reeds. They will see the python's approach, the mongoose's slink, long before you do. They will warn you. A warning for vines."

The drongos, whose entire survival strategy was based on early warning and aggressive defense, were silent. This was a language they understood. Not submission, but alliance. A trade of skills.

The lead drongo cocked its head. "And what does the King ask for in return?"

Bakul met its gaze. "When you give your warning cry for a python… let it be a cry all the loyal forest can understand. Be my sentinels. Let your voice become the voice of the Crown's watch."

A pact was sealed, not with a pledge of fealty, but with a mutually beneficial deal.

The drongos got superior hunting and an early-warning network. The weavers got safety and materials. Bakul got the most vigilant sentry system in the forest.

He returned to the *sal* tree that evening, his throat pouch full, but his spirit fuller. At the slit, he didn't just pass food. He whispered, "The web is singing, Bela. And I am learning its tune."

From the darkness, he heard the soft, contented tap of her beak against wood. It was the sound of approval.

Part 3:

The Heartwood Ascendant

Chapter 10:
The Pact of Roots and Rain

The first true monsoon downpour arrived not with a gentle patter, but with a deafening roar, as if the sky had split its seams. It hammered the leaves of the King's Sal, streamed in rivulets down the sealed entrance, and soaked Bakul to his skin as he clung to his sentinel branch. Inside, he knew, Bela was warm and dry, their chick—**Phalgun**—a growing ball of fluff and insatiable hunger.

The rain was a baptism for Bakul's fledgling network. He watched as his new alliances were stress-tested. The drongos, true to their word, used the storm's noise to mask their movement, becoming grey ghosts that darted from cover to cover, their sharp eyes missing nothing. The weaver birds had used the strong cliff-vines, and their nests swung wildly but held fast in the gale. From a nearby *bodhi* tree, Tal the woodpecker tapped out a rapid, coded message against a hollow limb: *"Python. West stream. Moving slow."* It was a message not just for Bakul, but for every creature in earshot who knew the code—a code Tal was now teaching to the mongooses and the alert junglefowl.

The web was holding. More than holding, it was vibrating with intelligence.

It was Tal who brought the final piece of the puzzle. As the storm abated to a steady drizzle, the great black woodpecker landed heavily beside Bakul, water flicking from his gleaming plumage. He didn't greet him. He simply stated: "The old king's last words. 'Heartwood Nest.' You have been thinking like a bird. Think like a tree."

Bakul, weary but alert, shifted. "It is a metaphor. The heart of the forest."

Tal made a dry, rattling sound of impatience. "Metaphors are for mynas and poets. My kind have been drumming on the bones of this forest since the first seed cracked. We listen to the stories in the grain." He jabbed his beak toward the north-west, where the deepest, oldest valleys lay shrouded in perpetual mist. "There is a tale, sung in the rings of the ancient ones, of a Gathering before all gatherings. A pact not just among birds, but with the forest itself. It was made in a place where the earth's breath is warm, and the roots drink from the first water."

"The First Tree," Bakul whispered, the legend stirring in his memory. A childhood fable.

"A Banyan," Tal confirmed. "Not just any Banyan. The Mother of Stranglers. Her aerial roots are like a hundred trunks; her canopy could shade a hill. The story says when the first rains fell after the pact, the leaders of every clan were anointed under her leaves. Their authority came not from the sharpest beak, but from the consent of the rain and the roots." Tal fixed him with his jet-black eyes. "Kala knows only the law of the talon.

But this… this is a law older than hornbills. If you are anointed there, in the season's first storm, your right to rule becomes part of the forest. His challenge becomes a blasphemy."

Hope, fierce and bright, flared in Bakul's chest. Then, practicality doused it. "If it's just a story, it's nothing. If it's real, Kala will seek it too. To destroy it. To prove nothing is sacred but strength."

"Exactly," Tal said. "It is a race. And you have an army he scorns."

From within the nest, Bela's voice, muffled but clear, came through the slit. "Then we must run it. And we must win."

Chapter 11: The Unsealing

The day Phalgun was to break the seal, the entire clearing held its breath. Bakul's coalition was present, not as a grand Parliament, but as a silent, watchful community. The weavers watched from their nests, the drongos from high, hidden perches, the squirrel family from a knot-hole. Even a gentle-eyed spotted deer stood at the tree line.

For two days, the sounds had been changing. No longer just the soft cheeps of a chick, but the determined, scrabbling *scratch-scratch-thump* of a beak against the dried mud from the inside. Bela was helping, weakening the wall.

Bakul perched directly before the slit. "Now, my heart," he whispered. "Now, my son."

With a final, cracking *crunch*, a piece of the seal fell away. A sliver of daylight pierced the dark chamber. Then, a tiny, black-and-white beak, curiously poking out. Then another crack, larger. And suddenly, the seal ruptured.

Bela emerged first. She blinked in the brilliant light, her feathers fluffing, her wings stretching for the first time in nearly four moons. She was thinner, her plumage less glossy, but her eyes were incandescent with triumph and maternal fire. She turned and gave a soft, encouraging *gok*.

And then he came. **Phalgun**. He tumbled more than stepped from the hole, a ball of awkward, fluffy down with wings too big for his body and a casque that was just a cute bump on his beak. He shook himself, sneezed, and let out a piping, confused cheep.

The assembled forest did not cheer. They simply… witnessed. The deer dipped its head. The squirrels chittered softly. It was a sacred moment.

Phalgun's eyes, the same bright amber as his father's, fixed on Bakul. He wobbled forward. Bakul leaned down, and gently, ever so gently, touched his beak to his son's. The greeting. The recognition.

"Welcome," Bakul rumbled, his voice thick with emotion. "Welcome to the Sundarban."

But the moment of peace was shattered by a harsh cacophony from above. Three of Kala's crows circled, their laughter like broken glass. "The heir emerges! Scrawny thing! Will it be a Take-Away Prince?"

Before Bakul could react, a streak of blue-black shot from the papyrus stand. A drongo, moving faster than sight, slammed into the lead crow, not with brute force, but with a sharp peck to its tail feather before twisting away. The crow squawked in surprise and pain. From the weaver colony, a chorus of angry chirps erupted, and a small but precise hail of dried mud pellets (a weaver's defense) peppered the other two crows.

The message was unmistakable. The king's allies were not just observers. They were defenders.

The crows fled, cawing insults but visibly shaken. Bakul looked from Bela's proud smile to the determined faces of his small allies. He had a family. He had an army. It was time to move.

Chapter 12: The Exodus

Preparing the exodus was an exercise in organized chaos that showcased Bakul's new style of leadership. There was no grand muster. Instead, the forest began to move in a coordinated whisper.

Tal the Woodpecker was the master of routes. He tapped out maps on hollow trees, showing the way through passes only his kind knew, avoiding Kala's known patrols. **The Drongo Pair** became the advance scouts and communications hub, their complex calls now carrying specific meanings: *"Clear path." "Ridge guarded." "Water ahead."* **The Weaver Colony**, in a stunning feat of collective engineering, wove strong, flexible carry-nets from grass and vine for the very young, the injured, and for transporting essential supplies of dried fruit and grubs.

They were joined by others. A troop of **langurs**, who remembered Garud's kindness and distrusted Kala's brutality, agreed to travel through the high canopy parallel to the birds, providing a noisy, distracting screen and extra eyes. A wise old **Indian rock python**, who cared only for the balance of the hunt and saw Kala's chaos as a threat to the game, offered to move unseen beneath them, a deterrent to any ground-based ambush from jackals or wild dogs in Kala's pay.

Bela and Phalgun flew at the center, protected by a rotating guard of the oldest, most loyal hornbill veterans. Bakul flew at the head, but he was not a solitary leader. He was the central node in a living network.

Their journey was a breathtaking, perilous panorama of the Western Ghats. They flew over mist-filled valleys where hornbills had never flown, their reflections skimming emerald tea plantations far below. They navigated narrow gorges where the winds howled like ghosts, the smaller birds tucking themselves into the slipstream of the larger ones. They drank from secret, crystal-clear waterfalls that cascaded down mossy cliffs.

And they faced trials. A forest fire, sparked by dry lightning, forced a desperate, night-time diversion, led by the heat-sensing pittas. A treacherous pass was found to be guarded by Kala's **shikras**, small but lethal falcons. Bakul didn't engage. He gave a signal.

The langurs in the trees above the pass began a tremendous racket, shaking branches and screaming as if a leopard was among them. As the shikras' attention was drawn upward, the main flock, led by the silent owls who had joined them, slipped through the shadows of the gorge below.

Phalgun, under Bela's watchful eye, thrived. His flights grew stronger, his landings less clumsy. He learned to listen for the drongo's warnings, to watch for Tal's coded taps. He was not just a prince on a journey; he was a student of the web.

Chapter 13: The Shadow in the Pass

The greatest test came at the **Crying Pass**, a wind-scoured defile of razor-sharp rock that was the only viable route to the valley of the First Tree. Tal had warned it was a perfect ambush site.

They were halfway through, the flock stretched in a long, vulnerable line, when the attack came. But it was not from the front or the sides.

It came from *above*.

Kala had enlisted the **brown fish owls**, massive, silent birds of the deepest night. They had been waiting, camouflaged against the grey rock of the overhanging cliffs. As the heart of the flock entered the pass, they dropped.

Silent as death, talons outstretched. They aimed not for Bakul, but for the center—for Bela and Phalgun.

A drongo's shriek of pure alarm echoed off the stone walls a second too late. Bakul turned, horror freezing his blood. He saw the descending shadows, saw Bela shove Phalgun behind her, raising her own beak in a futile, defiant slash.

Then, a streak of iridescent green and bronze shot from the flock, moving with suicidal speed. It was a **Malabar trogon**, a shy bird Bela had protected in her valley. It flew directly into the face of the lead owl, a burst of dazzling color and panic that made the owl veer off with a surprised hoot.

That moment of disruption was all that was needed. The python, lying unseen on a rock shelf, struck not to eat, but to *bludgeon*, its muscular body whipping out to knock another owl off course. The langurs, from the cliffs above, rained down a hail of stones and excrement.

But the owls were powerful. One broke through, its talons aiming for Phalgun.

Bakul was too far away. He cried out.

From within the protective cluster of older hornbills, a grey shape launched itself. It was **Vihanga**, the ancient elder who had proclaimed Bakul king. He was slow, his bones brittle. He placed himself between the talons and the prince.

There was a sickening thud. Vihanga fell, a spray of grey feathers floating in the dusty air of the pass. But his sacrifice had bought a second. Bela's beak found the owl's leg, and she bit down with all the fury of a sealed mother. The owl screamed, released Phalgun, and flapped away.

The ambush was broken. The owls, disoriented by the chaotic, multi-species defense, retreated.

In the sudden silence, broken only by the wind's cry, Bakul landed beside Vihanga. The old hornbill was breathing in ragged gasps, a deep wound in his side.

"My… king…" Vihanga whispered.
"You saved my son," Bakul said, his voice cracking.
"The line… must continue. For the… web." Vihanga's eyes found the distant, misty valley ahead. "Finish… the journey. Become… the Heartwood."

His eyes closed. The wind took his last breath.

They buried Vihanga under a cairn of stones in the pass that would henceforth bear his name. There was no time for lengthy mourning. But a new, hard resolve settled over the flock. They had bled for this future. They would see it born.

As they lifted off from the pass, Bakul flew beside Bela and a shaken but resolute Phalgun. Ahead, through the parting mists, they saw it.

Chapter 14: The First Tree

It was not a tree. It was a world.

The **First Tree** was a banyan of such staggering immensity that it seemed to hold up the sky itself. Its primary trunk was a wall of living wood, wider than a river. From its vast, sinuous branches, hundreds of aerial roots descended like stone columns in a cathedral, each one thick as an elephant, reaching down to plunge into the earth and become new trunks. Its canopy was a layered, green continent, hosting entire ecosystems of its own: ferns, orchids, cascading vines, and the nests of generations of birds. The air here was cool, thick with the scent of damp earth and ancient pollen, and hummed with a profound, deep silence.

It was the Heartwood Nest. Not a hollow, but the source.

As Bakul's weary, battle-scarred coalition settled into the surrounding trees and the forest floor below, a sense of awe stilled all chatter. Even Phalgun gazed up, his small beak agape.

But the awe was short-lived. From the opposite side of the great clearing, shadows detached themselves from the colossal roots. Kala had arrived first.

His forces were arrayed in stark, hierarchical order. His hornbills, big and battle-scarred, occupied the highest branches. Below them, the falcons and shikras. On the ground, sullen wild dogs and jackals lurked. Myna flitted nervously at Kala's side. They looked powerful, monolithic, and utterly contemptuous of the ragged, multi-species flock facing them.

Kala's voice boomed across the clearing, echoing in the natural amphitheater of roots. "You lead a carnival, nephew! A parade of beggars and weaklings! You come to this old place with stories? I come with the future!" He spread his wings. "This is the last gasp of the old ways. Look around you! The strong at the top. The useful below. The rest… gone. This is the natural order. The true Accord!"

Bakul flew forward, landing on a great arched root midway between the two armies. He did not spread his wings in challenge. He stood firm.

"You see a pyramid, Uncle," Bakul called, his voice carrying clear and calm. "I see a web. You see strength in talons. I see strength in connection. You offer a future where the drongo lives in fear of the shikra. I offer a future where the drongo's warning saves the shikra from the poacher's snare."

Myna shouted from behind Kala, "Pretty words! They won't stop a talon in your heart!"

"No," Bakul agreed, looking directly at his father's murderer. "But *this* will."

He raised his wing. It was not a signal to attack. It was a signal to *demonstrate.*

What happened next was not a battle. It was a symphony of interdependence.

As Kala's falcons, on his snarled command, dove for Bakul's seemingly vulnerable center, the drongos gave a specific, trilling cry. Instantly, the weaver birds, hidden in the ferns, released a cloud of sticky, seeded down that filled the air, blinding and confusing the diving hunters. The falcons pulled up, disoriented.

Kala snarled and sent his ground forces—the wild dogs—surging forward to attack the mammals with Bakul. But Tal the woodpecker, from a high root, tapped a frantic, staccato rhythm. The old rock python, along with two brothers who had joined the cause, uncoiled from the shadows of the root system, forming a living, hissing wall of muscle that made the dogs skid to a halt, yelping.

Enraged, Kala himself launched from his perch, a black arrow aimed at Bakul's heart. "Enough theatrics! I will end this myself!"

Bakul took to the air to meet him. This was the duel everyone had anticipated. Beak to beak. King vs. Usurper.

But Bakul did not fight to kill. He fought to deflect, to endure, to prove. They clashed in mid-air, a thunderous crack of beak on casque. They tumbled, locked together, towards the great root. Kala was stronger, fueled by a lifetime of bitter rage.

He pinned Bakul, his talon pressing on Bakul's wounded wing from the hornet attack long ago. Pain flared white-hot.

"You see?" Kala hissed, his breath foul. "This is the only truth! The strong on top!"

Bakul, straining, looked past Kala's looming head. He saw Bela, holding a terrified but fierce Phalgun back. He saw the drongos ready to suicide-dive, the langurs gathering rocks. He saw his web, ready to tear itself apart to save him. And he saw Myna, edging closer behind Kala, not to help his master, but with a sharp, pointed stone in his beak, his eyes fixed on the base of Kala's skull.

In that split second, Bakul understood Myna's endgame. He would let them weaken each other, then kill the winner and claim chaos.

As Kala raised his beak for a final, crushing strike, and Myna darted in, Bakul did the one thing no one expected. He used the last of his strength not to shove Kala away, but to *roll*, pulling Kala to the side.

Myna's sharp stone, aimed at Kala's neck, struck instead the hard root where Kala's head had been, sparking.

Kala, confused by the sudden movement, turned and saw Myna with the weapon, saw the murderous intent in his beady eyes. The betrayal was absolute, undeniable.

"You…" Kala roared.

In that moment of shattered trust, Bakul broke free. But he did not press his advantage. He stood, panting, between his uncle and the treacherous myna.

"This," Bakul gasped, blood on his beak, "is your natural order. Betrayal. Suspicion. The strong always watching their backs. Is that the kingdom you want? A kingdom where even your closest advisor is a knife in the dark?"

Kala looked from the cowering Myna to Bakul, who had just saved him from an assassin's blow. The simple, brutal logic of his world fractured. Strength had not saved him. Loyalty—a loyalty he had scorned—had.

The fight went out of him. His vast wings, which had cast such a long shadow, drooped. He looked at his own forces, held at bay not by a stronger army, but by a clever, cooperative one. He looked at the majestic, timeless First Tree, which seemed to judge his petty philosophy as the blink of a mayfly.

With a sound that was half-groan, half-sigh, Kala lowered his head. Not in defeat to Bakul, but in surrender to a greater truth.

It was then that the skies, which had been heavy and still, opened. The true monsoon rain, held back by the tension, began to fall. Not a storm, but a gentle, steady, blessing rain. It fell on the First Tree, on Bakul, on the bowed head of Kala, on Bela and Phalgun, on the drongos and the weavers, on every creature present.

The rain anointed them all. But it was Bakul who stood at the root, having fought not for domination, but for balance; not for victory over his uncle, but for the salvation of his family, both feathered and furred.

A single, pure note, from a hidden Malabar whistling thrush, pierced the patter of rain. Then another joined. And another. Until the entire clearing—both sides—was filled not with war cries, but with the rain-soaked, peaceful chorus of the Sundarban, whole once more.

Epilogue: The Whisper in the Canopy

The rain fell softly on the King's Sal, now not a fortress but a home. In the clearing below, the web had become a tapestry.

Bakul, his casque bearing a new, proud notch from the fight, watched as a young drongo practiced mock-dives on a patient, older hornbill guard—a drill that was now part of their shared defense. A woodpecker taught a family of squirrels the "snake-warning" tap code. At the stream, a painted stork stood guard while a junglefowl family drank, their ancient enmity softened by shared survival.

On the branch beside him, Bela preened Phalgun's now-glossy juvenile plumage. Their son was nearly full-grown, his own casque beginning to curve, his eyes alight with restless curiosity about the borders of the kingdom he would one day help rule.

"He asks to go to the Shadow Gorge," Bela murmured, her touch gentle. "To learn from his great-uncle."

Bakul watched a troop of langurs swing through the canopy, their route scouted ahead by a pair of friendly bulbuls. "Kala guards the dark places well," he said. "He has found a strength in purpose, not in power. Let Phalgun go. The web must include all threads, even the darkest ones."

That was the new Accord. Not a hierarchy from the Council Fig, but a dynamic, living network centered on the Heartwood—the First Tree, where Bakul and Bela now held court seasonally, listening to disputes, forging new pacts, always under the promise of the cleansing rain.

Myna was gone, exiled to the scorched edges of the forest, his whispers now empty against the chorus of cooperation. His fate was a lesson sung to every new brood: treachery unravels the web, and the web casts out what does not hold.

As the sun dipped below the Ghats, painting the sky in hues of orange and purple that matched Bakul's casque, he felt a deep, resonant peace. He was not just a king. He was a guardian. A node in the great, singing web of life. His father's last words were no longer a mystery. The Heartwood Nest was not a place to be *found*, but a truth to be *lived*: that the strength of the one is borrowed from the strength of the all.

Bela finished her preening and leaned her head against his shoulder, a comfortable, silent weight. Below them, the Sundarban breathed its evening sigh—a million rustles, chirps, calls, and taps, each one distinct, each one part of the whole.

It was not a perfect peace. There would always be Skin-Takers beyond the borders, storms within them, and the constant, beautiful struggle of life. But it was a living peace. A resilient one.

Bakul closed his eyes, listening to the forest his love had sealed, his allies had defended, and his family would inherit. It was the only story that mattered. The story of the web. And it was just beginning.

THE END

9 789374 061848

Printed at Repro India Ltd.